WELCOME TO

Collect the special coins in this book. You will earn one gold coin for every chapter you read.

Once you have finished all the chapters, find out what to do with your gold coins at the back of the book.

With special thanks to Conrad Mason

www.beast-quest.com

ORCHARD BOOKS

First published in Great Britain in 2017 by The Watts Publishing Group

1 3 5 7 9 10 8 6 4 2

Text © 2017 Beast Quest Limited.
Cover and inside illustrations by Steve Sims
© Beast Quest Limited 2017

Beast Quest is a registered trademark of Beast Quest Limited
Series created by Beast Quest Limited, London

A CIP catalogue record for this book is available from the British Library.

ISBN 978 1 40834 325 8

Printed in Great Britain

The paper and board used in this book are made from wood from responsible sources

Orchard Books
An imprint of Hachette Children's Group
Part of The Watts Publishing Group Limited
Carmelite House, 50 Victoria Embankment, London EC4Y 0DZ

An Hachette UK Company
www.hachette.co.uk
www.hachettechildrens.co.uk

Beast Quest®

RYKAR
THE FIRE HOUND

BY ADAM BLADE

ORCHARD

CONTENTS

They thought I was dead, but death is not always the end.

My body was consumed in Ferno's dragon-fire, though that pain is a distant memory now. I have been trapped in this place – this Isle of Ghosts – for too long. It is time for me to remind my old enemies of my power.

The boundary between the realm of spirits and the realm of the living is like a thick castle wall – unbreakable by force or magic. But every castle has its weakness – someone on the inside who can lower the drawbridge. And I have found him. A weak wizard, but strong enough to do my bidding.

Hear me, Berric! Heed my summons. Open the way for me to return, and I will show Avantia that Evil like mine is impossible to kill.

Malvel

TO THE SHARD MOUNTAINS

Kato's body felt cold and heavy in Tom's arms.

A breeze stirred the old man's long white beard, as Tom laid him down gently on the flagstones. He remembered the sneering face of Malvel. How the Dark Wizard had slain Kato, then fled like a coward.

Tom made a silent promise. *You won't go unavenged...*

"Is he...?" asked Elenna.

Tom nodded. "It's over."

As he said the words, the wizard's body began to twinkle with golden speckles of light. Then, slowly, it vanished into nothing. Only Kato's wooden staff was left.

Tom got to his feet, surveying the grey stone courtyard. Elenna stood nearby with Okira. The ogre towered five times as tall as Tom, with muscles like rocks and a head as big as a boulder. But as he knelt down beside Kato's staff, he looked like a lost, frightened child.

"This is not your fault," Tom said

to the ogre. *There's only one person
to blame for this…*

He turned to Elenna. "We have to
get to the Shard Mountains. Kato

said that Malvel would be heading that way. We have to stop him leaving the Isle of Ghosts."

The ogre shook his massive head. His voice rumbled like thunder in Tom's mind.

There is a dark and deadly Beast that lurks in the Shard Mountains... Malvel holds sway over him.

Tom nodded, feeling a squirm of unease. The Dark Wizard had stolen his father's amulet, the link between the spirit world and the world of the living. All Malvel needed was for this new Beast to give up his magical key. *Then he'll use it to escape the Isle of Ghosts and leave us stranded here for ever...*

"We'll need to cross the moat first," Tom said, gazing over towards the smashed drawbridge.

"The one that's full of acid?" asked Elenna, with an arched eyebrow.

"I didn't say it would be easy." Tom picked his way through fallen rubble to a gaping hole in the courtyard wall that Okira had made with his fists. Through it, he could see the moat seething and bubbling. Elenna came to join him. "Maybe I could carry you?" Tom suggested. "If I use the power of the golden boots, I might be able to jump across."

Elenna shook her head. "I don't know, Tom... It's a long way, even without me on your back."

Without speaking, Okira strode
to one of the guard towers set in
the courtyard walls. He turned and

pressed his back against the base
of the tower. Then with a growl he
began to push, muscles bulging.

"Rrrrrrraaaargh!"

Tom felt the stones of the
courtyard shake beneath his feet.
The tower groaned and shuddered.
Suddenly it gave way, collapsing into
the moat with a deafening clashing
of rocks. Plumes of acid splattered
all around. Tom flung up his shield
to protect himself and Elenna, and
he heard a sizzle as some liquid
splashed against it.

When the crashing died away, Tom
lowered his shield. The tower lay half
submerged in the moat, forming a
bridge across it. The acid hissed and

fizzed at the stone, but didn't seem to damage it at all.

The stone is from the Shard Mountains, rumbled Okira, wiping sweat from his brow. *It cannot be melted. Except by Rykar, so it is said.*

Tom placed his fingers against the red jewel in his belt, to speak to the ogre. *Who is Rykar?*

The Beast you seek to battle, said Okira. *Come. I will guide you.* He clambered up on to the wall of the fallen tower and pointed towards a cluster of dark peaks on the horizon. *That is where you must travel. The Shard Mountains!*

Tom and Elenna followed Okira along a worn track, across a barren, rocky plain. After half a day's travelling, they had left Kato's Castle far behind. In the distance, the mountains rose up like giant black teeth jutting crookedly into the gloomy sky.

The ogre frowned, and his voice rumbled with anger. *I have trodden this path many times. Malvel made me carry rocks from the mountains to rebuild the castle.*

When will we get there? asked Tom.

Soon – we must be patient, Okira replied. Suddenly, the ogre stumbled to a halt, groaning and clutching at his head with his great hands.

"What's wrong?" asked Elenna, drawing her bow.

Tom's hand closed on his sword hilt. He looked all around, but they were alone.

Evil magic, grunted Okira. *I can feel it! There is some enchantment on the road.*

"Is there some way past it?" said Tom.

Okira shook his head. *I can go no further*, he said. *I must return to the castle. It is my duty to guard it. Farewell, Master of the Beasts, and be careful.* Backing away, he raised a hand in farewell.

"Goodbye, Okira," Elenna said.

"And thank you," Tom added.

They watched the ogre turn and plod away, back to his lonely fortress home. Then they set off again towards the mountains.

The day wore on, and a chill wind

began to blow across the plain. It howled mournfully, making Tom and Elenna shiver.

"What's that up ahead?" asked Elenna suddenly.

Tom peered into the distance. His heart hammered as he spotted a hooded figure on the road, heading towards them. Tom drew his sword and shield. "Be ready," he said.

GHOST ON THE ROAD

"Is it Malvel?" asked Elenna, pulling an arrow from her quiver.

As Tom peered closer, he saw that the person looked too small to be the Dark Wizard. But something about the figure's long, loping strides was familiar...

He drew on the power of the

golden helmet. His vision sharpened magically until he could see the face under the hood as clearly as if it were a few feet away. Tom gasped. "It's Marc!"

Elenna lowered her arrow. "You mean Aduro's apprentice?" Her face had gone pale, and her eyes were wide.

Tom felt every bit as shocked as Elenna looked. Marc had been killed by Malvel when he was no older than Tom himself. *And here he is again. A lost soul, haunting the Isle of Ghosts...*

As Marc approached, he pulled back his hood. He looked just like he had done when he was alive – a scruffy young boy. Only his eyes were different – they looked much older, and they were glaring fiercely at Tom and Elenna.

"So, the 'great hero' has come to pay me a visit," snarled Marc, when he reached them. "How lucky I am!"

Tom's jaw dropped. "I'm sorry…" he began, but Marc shook his head.

"Save your apologies! You should have protected me, Tom. I died because of you. It's all your fault."

Tom couldn't meet the boy's eyes. "I failed you," he murmured. "I know that." His stomach twisted with guilt.

"Much good that does me!" snorted Marc. "It should have been you who died at Malvel's hands."

"Enough!" said Elenna. She stepped in between them, and Tom saw that the arrow was now fitted to her bowstring. "You're not real. You can't be! Marc was brave and noble. Not cruel and full of self-pity."

"You're no better than Tom!" shouted Marc. "Look at you, chasing glory while you let innocents die. Innocents like me! And Kato!"

"How do you know about that?" asked Elenna.

"He's right," said Tom softly. "We let Marc die, just like we did Kato."

"We did everything we could to save them both!" said Elenna. She turned on Marc. "All right... If you really are Aduro's apprentice, tell us this. Do you remember the time you cast that floating spell on Captain Harkman?"

"Of course I do!" Marc shot back.

Elenna smiled grimly. "That's funny," she said. "Because it never happened."

Tom felt a chill creep across his skin. *If that's not Marc, who is it...?*

The boy's face twisted into a savage scowl. Then he whipped a sharp, glinting dagger from inside his robes and leapt at Elenna.

Tom darted in front of his friend, throwing up his shield just as the knife came flashing down. The blade glanced off it. He drew his sword, but when he lowered his shield to strike, he saw that Marc had vanished.

"Looking for someone?" sneered the boy's voice, from behind.

Tom whirled round just in time to

see the dagger come slicing down at his throat. He managed to get his arm up and grab Marc's wrist, straining to push it away. But Marc seemed to have magical strength and the blade inched slowly towards Tom's neck.

With a grunt, Tom bent low and heaved the boy up and over his head. Marc rolled and scrambled to his feet, still clutching the dagger.

"Get back!" shouted Elenna. Tom dived away, landing heavily on his shield. He rolled over just in time to see Elenna loose her arrow.

Whhhhhsshh!

The arrow flew straight at Marc's chest. But as it struck, the figure turned into a swirl of black smoke and the arrow passed straight through. Tom watched in horror as a new face appeared in the smoke. The cold, evil eyes of Malvel stared at him.

"This is only the beginning, Tom," said Malvel. "I'll be waiting for you, up in the quarry of the Shard Mountains. If you dare to face me, that is!"

The last thing Tom heard was the Dark Wizard's savage laughter, before the wind carried the black smoke away and left no trace of Marc, or Malvel, behind.

"Are you all right?" asked Elenna, helping Tom to his feet.

Tom shook himself, and nodded. "Come on," he said. "If Malvel thinks we're not brave enough to face him, he'd better think again."

THE LIVING AND THE DEAD

Dusk was falling by the time they reached the mountains. Tom and Elenna clambered up over the dark rocks into a shadowy pass which ran between two steep hillsides. The wind kept blowing, buffeting them mercilessly.

Tom shivered and tried to focus

on following the rocky road. But he couldn't help thinking about how Marc had blamed him for what had happened. It wasn't just the guilt which made him uneasy. *That might have been the first of Malvel's tricks, but it won't be the last... We're walking into danger.*

But how else could they stop the Dark Wizard?

"Look – we've reached the end of the road," said Elenna, pointing up ahead. Sure enough, the trail led to a steep, ragged mountainside. A huge expanse of rock had been quarried away, leaving giant boulders strewn below.

"This must be where Okira got all

the stone to build Kato's Castle," said Tom.

"So what do we do now?" asked Elenna. "I don't see Malvel anywhere – or this Rykar, either."

Tom picked his way among the fallen rocks to the foot of the quarried mountainside. A glint in one of the boulders caught his eye, and he peered closer. The stone was as black as obsidian and slightly see-through. He gasped.

There's something inside it…

Kneeling, Tom rubbed at the dusty surface of the rock until he could see the object encased deep within.

"I think it's a claw!" he murmured.

Elenna knelt at his side. "It must

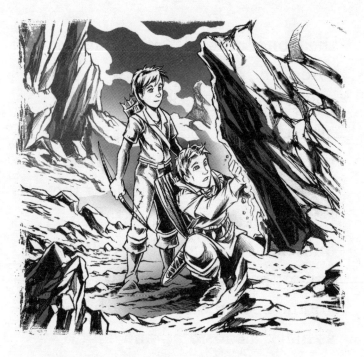

be the key," she said, her eyes
widening. "We did it, Tom! We got
here before Malvel."

Tom's heart was racing. *Is this too
easy?* He shook his head and drew
his sword. "Stand back," he said. "I'll
cut it out." He raised the blade and

brought it down as hard as he could.

CLANG!

Tom's sword bounced off the black rock, the hilt juddering in his hand.

"Use the power of the golden breastplate," suggested Elenna.

Tom drew on the magic and felt the muscles in his arms tingle with a sudden surge of strength. He raised the sword and swung it down again.

CLAAAANG!

Once again, the blade rebounded off the rock.

Tom frowned at the claw. *How are we supposed to get it out of there?*

"This is a battle that you can't win, Tom."

The voice didn't belong to Elenna. But it was one that Tom knew well. A voice which filled his heart with warmth and with sorrow, all at once. He whirled around.

Sitting on a rock nearby was a tall, strong-looking man with a beard, long golden hair and kind brown eyes. He smiled, and Tom felt a rush of joy.

"Father..." he said.

Taladon the Swift nodded, his eyes glinting. "I'm glad I have got to see you, just once more."

"Be careful," said Elenna, in a low voice. "This could be another of Malvel's tricks."

The thought almost broke Tom's

heart, but he knew his friend was right. He swallowed hard. "Who are you really?" he asked.

The man frowned. "I'm your father, Tom."

"Prove it," said Tom. "When you were a child, you had an old wolfhound who went everywhere at your side. What was her name?"

A wistful look came over Taladon's face, and he sighed. "Oh, Tom... It's been so long, I had almost forgotten. We named her Jester, because everyone smiled when they saw her."

It's really him! Tom dropped his sword and shield and ran to his father. But Taladon held out a hand in warning. "No! Remember, you

must not touch me, my son."

Tom skidded to a halt, his heart aching.

"You're one of the living," said Taladon. "And I am one of the dead.

If you touched me, I would absorb some of your life force, just as Malvel did to Berric and you. It would make me stronger, but you would be weaker."

Tom had a sudden thought. "So if you were strong enough, you could return to the land of the living?" he asked.

Taladon nodded. "I could, but it would not be right. The dead should stay here, on the Isle of Ghosts. They should never return."

"Who says so?" said a voice from above.

Tom looked up. A cloaked figure stood on a rock above the quarried mountainside, silhouetted against the gloomy sky. Malvel sneered down at them. His long robe flapped in the wind, and his eyes blazed with triumph. "How foolish you are, Taladon," he said. "No wonder you will be stuck, festering here for ever, whilst I return to take my revenge on Avantia!"

"I'll die before I let that happen!" shouted Tom.

Malvel threw back his head and laughed. "That can be arranged, Master of the Beasts!" He flung out a hand, pointing to a dark cave mouth in the mountainside opposite the quarry. "Behold your doom... The last Beast you will ever face. Rykar the Fire Hound!"

Tom snatched up his sword and

shield, and turned to face the cave. Elenna ran to his side, drawing an arrow from her quiver.

"Run away, both of you!" said Taladon. "Please! It's too dangerous."

A rumbling growl sounded from the darkness within the cave. Then something stirred inside – a huge, shadowy shape. Tom, Elenna and Taladon all froze in horror, as the Beast began to emerge.

First came a glimpse of bared teeth, yellow and dripping with saliva. Next, a short, powerful snout and huge, staring eyes as white as bone appeared. Then the Beast's whole bulk prowled out into the twilight.

It was a giant dog, coated in thick

black fur, muscles rippling along his flanks, his legs and back lined with sharp, cruel spikes. Another growl sounded from deep inside Rykar's chest, and he pawed the ground,

scattering rocks with claws as long as
scythe blades.

"Prepare to join your father, Tom,"
jeered Malvel. "Rykar...tear them to
pieces!"

4

FIGHTING FIRE

The hound crept towards Tom and Elenna, his lips drawn back in a vicious snarl.

"I don't understand," hissed Elenna. "Why is the Beast doing what Malvel wants?"

"It's like Okira said," Tom replied. "Malvel must have some kind of control over Rykar." *But how?*

With a sudden bark the Beast lunged forward, drool spilling from his jaws. Tom and Elenna dived away from each other, out of Rykar's path. The Beast veered towards Tom, and a burst of flame spewed from his open mouth, bathing the mountainside in blood-red light.

Tom flung his shield in front of him, just in time. Heat rippled around the edges of it, making him feel as though he were standing next to Uncle Henry's forge. But the magic of Ferno's scale, set in the surface of his shield, kept the flames at bay.

That was close!

The fire-breath died and Tom darted away. He wiped sweat from his brow. A curtain of smoke lingered in the air, and Tom could see Rykar's white eyes through the fumes, hunting for him.

Tom rushed through the haze, slicing his sword down at the creature's massive head. But a huge black paw swiped the blade away. Tom stumbled to a halt, and as the smoke cleared, he saw the Beast towering over him. Rykar sniffed hungrily at Tom, as though he were a joint of roasted meat.

"Get down!" shouted Elenna, and Tom ducked low as one of her arrows whizzed through the darkness and glanced off the Beast's side.

Rykar howled and leapt towards Elenna, swinging his tail round like a club. The wall of black-furred muscle hit Elenna with a sickening thud, lifted her off her feet and knocked her sprawling on to the rocks. There was a snapping sound as she fell, and Tom saw that she'd landed on her bow and broken it in two.

"Careful, Tom!" shouted Taladon through the smoke, and Tom saw Rykar turning on him, opening his jaws. Another stream of flame burst out.

Tom dived behind a boulder. He could feel the fire heating the stone, and heard cracking and bubbling as it melted. *If those flames hit me even once, it's all over...*

The fire fizzled out and Tom leapt from his hiding place, shield in front of him. Rykar was gone. A slavering mouth lunged at him from the side, through the haze of smoke. Tom threw up his shield and a huge, matted snout smashed into it, barging him back. Rykar stalked around Tom, snapping his jaws. *He's just toying with me!*

The Beast's great paw came swiping round again, crashing into Tom's shield and shoving him sideways. Tom staggered, tripped on a rock and had to roll away.

He looked around, and saw Elenna still picking herself up. His father stood a little way off, jaw clenched. "You can do this, Tom!" Taladon shouted, and Tom felt a rush of energy.

It's up to me to defeat this Beast. Maybe if I could get to higher ground, somehow...

Tom dashed over to a stack of boulders and began to climb, using his sword to steady himself as he clambered to the top of the rocks. Turning back, he saw Rykar coming for him, head lowered like a charging bull.

CRRAAASH! Rykar struck the rocks, making them shudder. Tom stumbled, only just managing not to fall off. Then the fire hound seized the biggest of the boulders in his jaws, and with one savage movement he crushed it to dust.

Tom felt the pile of rocks give way beneath him. He leapt into the air to stop himself getting crushed, but he landed awkwardly on the pieces of broken stone, falling on to his side with a yelp of pain.

The Beast loomed over him, darker than the night sky, a growl rolling at the back of his throat. A gust of stinking breath made Tom wrinkle his nose and almost retch.

A glint to his left caught his eye. Something glimmered among the

blackened pieces of the rocks that
Rykar had melted with his breath.

The claw!

It was lying there, out in the open.
Tom tried to rise, but a massive
paw came slamming down on to his
shoulder, pinning him to the rocks

with incredible force. Tom squirmed, but Rykar held him in place. The Beast lowered his head till Tom could smell his rancid fur, and look deep into the milky emptiness of his huge white eyes.

"He's hungry, Tom," purred Malvel. Tom couldn't see the wizard from where he lay, but he could hear the cruel triumph in his enemy's voice. "I expect you've been wondering how I persuaded the fire hound to do my bidding? It's simple, really. I promised him something in return... the flesh of a Master of the Beasts! The only question is, will Rykar eat you raw? Or will he roast you alive first? I can't wait to find out!"

The Beast opened his mouth, yellow teeth coming closer and closer...

Something barged into the Beast's foreleg, and for an instant the crushing pressure on Tom's chest lifted. He sucked in a deep breath of air. Then there were hands on his shoulders, and someone pulled him clear, dragging him across the rocks, away from the Beast's grasp.

His rescuer let him go, and Tom saw that it was Taladon. Relief flooded his heart. But his father's face was ashen. "I'm sorry, my son..." he whispered.

"You saved my life..." Tom began. Then he felt his limbs being overcome by a heavy feeling, as though he were falling asleep. At the same time he saw colour spread through his father's cheeks, making him look young and strong again.

"By touching you I've drained some of your life force," said Taladon. "I'm so sorry..."

"You had no choice," said Tom. As he spoke, he looked down at his own body – it seemed to flicker for an instant, as though he were becoming a ghost himself.

Malvel's harsh laughter rang out, echoing from the rocks.

"I hate to interrupt this tender moment," he sneered. "But I'm afraid, Taladon, you've only made your son's

suffering worse. Now Tom can watch his little friend die, before he follows her into the Beast's jaws!"

Tom felt a cold weight settle in

his stomach. *Elenna!* He tried to sit up, but the movement drained all his energy at once and he fell back, panting.

Turning his head, he saw that Rykar was prowling across the rocks, herding Elenna back against the mountainside. Without her bow, she had nothing but a quiver of arrows to defend herself with. She drew one and hurled it at the Beast, but it only bounced off his muscled shoulders.

Elenna stumbled to a halt with her back against a sheer rock face. There was nowhere left to run.

5

THROUGH THE PORTAL

"Get away, you overgrown mutt!" Elenna yelled at the Beast. Rykar leaned closer, jaws gaping wide, ready to burn her to ashes with his breath...

Tom tried to stand, but his body felt as though it was made out of lead, and he sank back down again.

I can't help her!

Suddenly Tom felt his shield yanked off his arm.

"Leave this to me," said Taladon. Before Tom could stop him, his father raced across the rocks with the shield, his body moving faster than before, powered with the energy he had taken from Tom. He dived in front of Elenna, holding out the shield to shelter them both.

Whhhhhhsssssh!

A jet of flame shot from Rykar's throat and slammed into the shield, spilling round the edges and scorching Taladon's arms and legs.

"Stop!" Tom screamed.

But fire kept pouring from the

Beast's mouth. Tom could see his
father's hair singeing, his trousers
and boots turning black with soot.
But Taladon stood firm, protecting
Elenna from the blaze. She tried to
get past, but Tom's father stood in
front of her, shielding her from harm.

"No..." Tom pleaded, but there was nothing he could do. *I can't watch him die all over again...*

At last, the flames died in Rykar's mouth and the Beast edged backwards.

Tom's father fell to his knees. His whole body was smoking. Elenna rushed to him, but Taladon thrust at her with his hands. "Away!" he croaked. His clothes were scorched and tattered, and his skin was blotched red with burns.

"Malvel!" howled Tom. Rage stirred in his heart, and he clenched his fists as tight as he could. "You won't get away with this!"

"Oh, but I will," came the wizard's

cold voice. Tom's enemy had climbed down the mountainside and stood by the ruins of the obsidian rock. Malvel bent to pick up the claw and raised it high, a savage grin painted on his face. "Rykar, down!" he called. The Beast obediently lay flat, and Malvel clambered on top, using fistfuls of black fur to pull himself up. He settled behind the Beast's head, as though Rykar were a stallion. "It is over for you, Tom! I have the key now, and I won't be staying on the Isle of Ghosts a moment longer. You, on the other hand...well, I'm afraid you're stuck here."

Tom's eyes filled with angry tears as he watched the Dark Wizard draw out something small, glinting with silver. The Amulet of Avantia. Malvel held the claw against it, and at once there was a blinding flash of light.

Blinking, Tom saw that the night sky had been torn apart. A pure white doorway opened up in the darkness, bathing the mountainside in a cold, pale glow.

The portal to Avantia!

Malvel sighed. "You don't know how long I've waited for this, Tom! The day I would return to take revenge on the Kingdom of Avantia, and all the worthless peasants who live there. Goodbye, Tom. I would like to say you have been a worthy

adversary...but in the end you are just what you have always been. A weak, pathetic little boy!"

Malvel patted Rykar's flank, and the hound crouched low, ready to spring up into the shimmering rift of white light. Tom struggled to stand, but again he fell back, panting.

Malvel's right. I'm as helpless as—

THUNK!

A rock as big as a fist arced through the air and struck the Dark Wizard hard on his head. Malvel wobbled and slid off Rykar's back, landing in a heap. His eyes closed and a trickle of blood dribbled from his temple.

Tom turned to see where the rock had come from. *Elenna!* She stood at Taladon's side, hefting a second rock in her hand. She saw Tom looking at her, and shrugged. "I don't need a bow to teach Malvel a lesson."

The fire hound sprang up, launching his night-black body towards the white crack in the sky. "No!" shouted Tom, but it was too late. With a whip of his tail, the Beast disappeared through the doorway.

We need to go after him!

Tom looked round to where Taladon lay on the ground. Smoke still rose from his back. "We need to get him to Daltec. He can save him, I know it."

Taladon raised his head, peering between sweat-soaked strands of hair. "No, Tom," he said. "It's over."

His voice was a dry croak. Elenna took him by the arms, propped him up and dragged him to Tom's side. There Taladon sank to his knees again, reached out and held Tom's ghostly hands in his own scorched ones.

"You must leave," he whispered. "You must forget me, and you must never come back."

"I can't," said Tom, his voice cracking.

Taladon smiled – a smile that made Tom's heart clench with pain.

"Don't grieve for me, son," said Taladon. "I am the proudest father who ever lived. Now at last I can pass on from the Isle of Ghosts,

knowing what a fine Master of
the Beasts you have become. Go!
Protect Avantia, as you've sworn to
do."

Taladon pointed towards the
portal, and Tom saw that the crack
of white light was shrinking,
gradually closing up.

"Your father's right, Tom," said

Elenna quietly.

"Very well," whispered Tom, his gaze still fixed on his father's face. "I will go. I will protect the kingdom."

Taladon smiled again. He let out a long, contented sigh. Then Tom felt his father's hands melting into thin air. "Stay," he pleaded. "Just for—"

But Taladon was gone, his spirit dissolved into nothingness.

A groan of despair leaked from Tom's throat, unbidden.

"I'm so sorry," whispered Elenna.

"Don't be," said Tom, firmly. "Like my father said – we have a kingdom to save."

As he spoke the words, he felt a fresh energy surging through his body. He looked down and saw that his flesh had become solid again. *The energy Taladon absorbed from me – it's mine once more!*

Tom snatched up his shield and leapt to his feet. Above, the portal had dwindled into almost nothing. "Come on," he said. "For Avantia!"

He began to climb the rocky mountainside, followed by Elenna. Soon they had clambered up level with the portal. All it would take was one good jump...

"This is not the end..." croaked a voice.

Tom looked down and saw Malvel lying on the ground, eyes half open, and holding the lump on his head.

"We'll meet again, Tom," said Malvel. "Sooner than you think."

"We'll defeat you," said Tom. "Like we always have."

With that, he and Elenna launched themselves from the mountain. Side by side, they plunged into the light.

6

HUNTING GROUND

For a moment, whiteness filled Tom's vision, forcing his eyes shut. He felt as though he was falling at incredible speed, his body battered by fierce winds on all sides. Then, with a jolt, he was still.

When he opened his eyes, he was standing beside Elenna on a

flat hilltop. A pale morning sun lit up gently swaying grass, and a gentle breeze ruffled their hair and tunics. Looking round, Tom saw rolling green fields below, and some distance to the north, the city where they had begun their Quest, its rooftops shimmering in the sunshine.

"Avantia!" said Elenna, smiling. "It feels good to be back. And look, the amulet brought us to the top of the Knight's Knoll."

Tom heard a whinny and hoofbeats approaching up the steep side of the knoll.

"Storm!" said Tom, and his heart leapt. *He must have been waiting*

for us the whole time we were away!
Tom raced to the edge of the hilltop,
eager to see his stallion again. But
when the horse came galloping
into view, he stopped in his tracks.

Storm's eyes were wide and staring with fear, and flecks of soot flew off his mane as he ran.

"Rykar's attacked Storm!" said Elenna. She patted the horse's neck. "Lucky our old friend was fast enough to get away."

The stallion nuzzled up to Tom. "It's so good to see you again," Tom murmured, stroking Storm's forehead.

"Look!" gasped Elenna, pointing down the steep slope of the Knight's Knoll. Great gouges were torn in the mud below, as though by the claws of some huge creature. Tom peered closer, following the churned-up tracks away from the foot of the knoll, heading north...

Towards the City.

"We've got to catch him," said Tom. "Before he reaches King Hugo's palace!"

Tom and Elenna clambered on to Storm's back. The stallion reared up with a snort, then set off at a gallop, flying down the hillside. Tom couldn't help grinning at the feel of the wind in his hair. Storm's hooves thundered on the ground, carrying them down the Knoll, across a grassy field and through a ragged copse of trees.

"There he is!" shouted Elenna, pointing up ahead.

The giant black hound looked

even bigger in the morning light, wider than a cart. His tail lashed as he bounded over the fields.

"Catch him, Storm!" whispered Tom, digging his heels into the flanks of his loyal steed.

As the stallion sped up, someone spoke inside Tom's head.

I sense you, Master of the Beasts...

The soft, growling voice made Tom's skin crawl. It was Rykar, speaking through the red jewel.

I have lived in the shadows for too long, hissed Rykar. *Avantia will be my hunting ground... I will sate my hunger on human flesh, and I will be more powerful than ever before!*

"Not while there's blood in my

veins," muttered Tom. They were gaining ground, drawing level with the racing Beast. "Take the reins," he told Elenna, swinging both legs to one side of Storm's neck.

"What are you going to—?" began Elenna.

Tom launched himself through the air.

For a horrifying moment, he thought he had missed, but his hands found Rykar's back and he clung on, clutching fistfuls of black fur. He felt his body jerk back as the Beast jolted forwards.

Let go of me! Rykar raged.

Tom held on tight. He tried to push a leg up over the Beast's back,

but Rykar bucked suddenly, and
Tom felt himself twisting away.
The fur slipped through his fingers,
and he dropped to the ground,

curling into a ball as he bounced and sprawled on the muddy grass. He lay flat for a moment, catching his breath, trying to ignore a pulsing pain in his ribs.

"Tom!" shouted Elenna.

Looking up, Tom saw his friend streaking ahead on Storm, with the Beast galloping not far behind. "Get to the palace!" Tom yelled. "Tell them to raise the drawbridge!"

Elenna nodded and crouched down low. She flicked the reins and Storm sped up, outpacing Rykar. Soon both the horse and the hound were gone, distant dots flying across the fields towards the City.

Tom scrambled to his feet,

clutching his ribs. None of them were broken, but when he took a step forward, pain shot through his ankle. *Just a sprain.* Elenna would get to the City before Rykar, but Tom had to get there too. The last words of his father ran through his mind, filling him with courage.

Protect Avantia, as you've sworn to do...

He closed his eyes and drew on the power of the golden leg armour. The magic came at once, surging into his legs. Then he began to run.

The sprain seemed like a distant memory as he raced across the field and leapt over a hedgerow. Trees, streams and farmhouses whipped by on either side of him. He barely glanced at them. His gaze was fixed on the giant claw-mark tracks of the Beast, intertwining with Storm's hoof prints.

The sun rose as Tom ran onwards, never stopping, until at last he crested a rise and saw the City up ahead. Its white walls shone in the midday sunshine. Above, the turrets of King Hugo's palace seemed to pierce the clouds.

Tom ran on through the city gates. He darted along cobbled streets past surprised onlookers, turned a corner and skidded to a halt at the edge of the moat.

The castle walls were thronging

with soldiers, their armour glinting as they raced to and fro, loading catapults with heavy-looking barrels. Tom spotted Captain Harkman among them, bellowing orders as he helped load the catapults.

Tom scanned the wall and saw to his relief that the drawbridge had been pulled up. *Elenna must have got here first!* Then a low, vicious growl to his left made him whirl around.

Rykar stood by the moat, the fur pricked up all along his arched back. He had one paw raised, as though he were about to lunge forward, and he was glaring up at the walls. His lips were curled in a snarl.

Why doesn't he attack? Tom

wondered. Then he realised. *The fire hound can't swim! He can't cross the moat...*

Tom drew his sword and crouched down, ready for battle. "Rykar!" he called. "You'll never enter the palace. Not without facing me first!"

Rykar turned his glowing, moon-like eyes on Tom. He let out a bark which sounded almost like a laugh. *You think you can stop me, Master of the Beasts?*

The fire hound lowered his head, and a gout of flame erupted from his jaws, surging across the surface of the moat. There was a sizzling, hissing sound as clouds of steam rose into the air, so much that Tom had to

duck down behind his shield. When
he looked again, the moat was still
boiling and bubbling, and steam was
still rising.

Rykar unleashed another torrent
of flame, then another, all the water
in the moat boiling away to nothing.

The Beast charged down into the
dried-up bed through the steam and
smoke, and slammed into the castle
wall.

THUD!

The wall groaned with the impact.
Tom remembered the way Okira the

ogre had toppled the tower in Kato's Castle, and the blood ran cold in his veins.

Rykar's going to smash the wall to pieces!

Sure enough, Rykar threw himself against it a second time, and a third. *THUD! THUD!* Then a deafening series of crashes rang out, mingling with the yells of Captain Harkman's men as the wall collapsed in a cloud of falling masonry.

Rykar leapt over the rubble, pouncing into the castle courtyard.

Moments later, Tom heard screams.

7

FIRE AND ICE

I've got to stop that Beast!

Tom raced down into the dried-up moat and leapt over the ruins of the castle wall. He landed in a crouch in the courtyard.

Chaos reigned, with soldiers running everywhere, shouting at each other and trying to herd civilians to safety. The stable roof was ablaze, belching out black smoke, and above it loomed Rykar. His head swayed as he spat out another searing jet of flame, setting fire to a wagon stacked with spears.

"Now!" came a shout from above. Looking up, Tom saw that Captain Harkman had ordered the catapults on the walls to be turned inwards. They let fly, launching burning barrels like comets into the courtyard.

Tom watched as the barrels arced through the air and struck Rykar's flanks, exploding with showers of sparks. They made no more impact than a child tossing pebbles at an angry bull. *The Beast is invulnerable to fire,* Tom realised, as the flames sizzled and died away.

Rykar let out another vicious growl and snatched up a sheep, which kicked and squirmed until he devoured it in one bite.

"Arrows!" Tom shouted up at the wall. Harkman saw Tom and nodded. He gestured to his archers, and the bowmen let fly with a hail of arrows, whizzing and zipping towards the Beast in a deadly, flashing storm.

Rykar whined as the missiles struck home, sticking into him like a hedgehog's spines. But he simply shook himself and the arrows fell free, clattering on the ground among the wreckage of the barrels.

Captain Harkman looked desperately down at Tom. *That's all he's got...so now it's up to me!*

Tom darted across to the burning wagon full of spears. He plucked

one free, still alight. Drawing on the strength of his golden breastplate, he hurled it with deadly force at the Beast.

THUNK!

The burning spear lodged deep

in Rykar's leg. The massive hound let out a bloodcurdling howl and rounded on Tom, white eyes wide and staring. *You, Master of the Beasts*, snarled Rykar. *Your human flesh will be the first I taste!*

Tom crouched down behind his shield, sword poised to strike. "Harkman!" he called, without taking his eyes off the Beast. "Get everyone inside."

As Harkman and his soldiers hurried to get the last of the townsfolk into the safety of the castle, Tom watched the fire hound. Hackles had risen all along Rykar's back, and he stalked towards Tom, a string of smoking drool dangling from each curved yellow fang.

Out of the corner of his eye, Tom saw two familiar figures running towards him in the shadow of the castle wall. Elenna had slung a new bow from the armoury over her shoulder. Her companion was a tall young wizard, stumbling under the weight of an enormous open spell book, ancient pages flapping as they ran.

"Daltec!" said Tom, as his two friends joined them.

"What a relief to see you, Tom," gasped the wizard, bending over to catch his breath. "I feared that your journey to the Isle of Ghosts might have been your last Quest!"

"It still might," said Elenna, pointing at Rykar. "Unless we do something about that fire hound. And fast!"

"Ah yes," said Daltec, straightening his hat. "I have a spell we can use against him. I'll just need your sword…"

Tom offered him the blade. But before Daltec could do anything, Rykar lurched forward, jaws snapping hungrily.

Flinging out his shield, Tom met the full force of Rykar's snout. *CRUNCH!* His arm trembled and he staggered backwards, a sharp pain stabbing through his sprained ankle. *It feels like being hit by a*

farmer's cart! "Back!" he shouted.
He sheltered his friends as they
retreated, until they were up against
the outer wall of the palace.

He's trying to trap us! Tom
realised. But it was too late.

"No escape," said Daltec, his voice
hoarse.

"The spell," said Tom. "Whatever
you were going to do, Daltec, do it
now!"

But the wizard was transfixed by
the huge white eyes of the Beast as
he prowled closer and closer...

Suddenly, Elenna rushed forward
and picked up one of the metal
hoops from among the broken bits
of barrel on the ground. Rykar's

jaws parted to unleash a burst of
flame at her, but she pivoted on
one foot, whipping the metal hoop
around. Just as Tom understood
what she was doing, she swung the
hoop expertly over the Beast's snout,

trapping the jaws together.

The Beast shook his head frantically, but he couldn't dislodge the metal that held his mouth closed.

Go, Elenna!

"Well done!" called Daltec.

"It won't hold for long!" shouted Elenna.

Tom ran to join her, sifting through the broken barrels to find more hoops, until they had three held together. Rykar was still shaking his head and pawing at the hoop. Tom watched closely, waiting for just the right moment. Then he and Elenna rushed in and together they pushed all three hoops on to Rykar's snout, before dodging back out of range of the Beast's heavy, swiping paws.

"Quickly," said Tom, holding out his sword for Daltec as Rykar thrashed furiously. "Cast the spell!"

Daltec laid a hand on Tom's blade and began to read from the spell book, muttering strange words under his breath.

The blade shimmered, and turned icy blue. Then a fierce chill shot through Tom's palm and into his arm, so cold it numbed him to the bone. He let out a gasp.

"That should do it," said Daltec, stepping back. Tom held up the sword, staring at its frosted metal surface in wonder. His fingers felt as though they had frozen around

the hilt, as though he couldn't let go,
even if he wanted to.

"Look out, Tom!" shouted Elenna.

Whirling round, Tom saw Rykar snorting flames from his nostrils, smoke rising from his snout. The air shimmered all around, and the iron hoops were dripping, melting with the fearsome heat of Rykar's breath. *It's not possible...* But the next moment, the fire hound forced his jaws open.

Drops of molten metal splattered the courtyard and, with a horrifying howl, Rykar spewed a torrent of flame straight at Tom's face...

THE HERO'S TOUCH

"Use the sword, Tom!" Daltec yelled.

With a split second to spare, Tom swung his blade round and met the flames surging towards him.

HHHHHISSSSSSSS!

Rykar's breath struck the metal with an icy hiss. Tom felt tremors pass through the hilt into his arm,

and he gripped tighter. He watched
in astonishment as the flames
seemed to disappear into the sword,
leaving nothing but steam and
smoke billowing into the air. It was
like plunging a red-hot blade into
a bucket of water back at Uncle

Henry's forge. *Except this time it's the sword that's cold, and Rykar's breath that's hot!*

The Beast let out a furious growl, then his chest puffed up as he got ready to breathe out another gout of flame...

Not this time, Rykar!

Tom plunged through the steam and the smoke, swinging his icy blue blade. Rykar was just as fast, bringing up a paw and meeting the sword with his claws. *CLANG!* But Tom kept up the attack, hacking and slashing at the Beast, with Rykar parrying every blow.

Then the fire hound sprang forward, barging into Tom and

knocking him on to his back.

"Tom!" shouted Elenna. But it was too late – Rykar's jaws gaped wide, curved teeth ready to plunge down into Tom's flesh.

It's over, Master of the Beasts, snarled Rykar's triumphant voice.

"That's right," Tom murmured, through gritted teeth. "Over for you!"

Drawing on all his strength, Tom drove his sword up into the Beast's neck. He felt the blade shudder to a halt as it lodged in Rykar's flesh.

For an instant, the Beast's eyes widened, milky pools gazing at Tom in shock. Then Tom felt a rush of cold spread through his blade and

out into Rykar, crackling across the
Beast's body and transforming him,
inch by inch, into a glistening blue
statue.

I've turned Rykar to ice!

A wave of freezing air washed
over Tom. Then cracks began to

spread across the fire hound.

"Look out!" shouted Captain Harkman, from somewhere above. But there was no time to get away. Tom closed his eyes as the Beast crumbled into a thousand shards of ice, burying Tom in freezing darkness.

"Tom? Can you hear us?"

The distant voice was muffled.

Tom tried to speak, to call out.
Panic closed over his chest. He
couldn't breathe.

"He's in there somewhere!" cried Elenna. Tom could see her shadow moving through the mound of ice weighing down on him. He wanted to call out to her, but the cold had seeped into his joints, until he was so numb that he could hardly move a muscle.

Soldiers joined Elenna, shovelling away with their spears and shields, until at last Elenna and Daltec were able to reach in, grab Tom beneath his arms and drag him free. Ice fell from Tom's bruised body as he rose. He gasped, shivering. His tunic was damp as he stepped stiffly down on to the paving stones. Gradually the blood began to flow through his limbs again, and he rubbed at his arms to keep warm.

Aduro pushed his way through the soldiers who thronged all around.

"Goodness, Tom!" he said. "You really know how to make an entrance, don't you?"

Tom couldn't help grinning. He almost flung his arms around his old friend, then remembered how cold and wet he was, and held himself back.

Aduro fixed him with a stern gaze. "You should never have gone to the Isle of Ghosts, Tom," he said. "It was foolish." His mouth twitched into a smile. "Foolish...and brave. Just the sort of adventure your father,

Taladon, would have loved."

At the mention of his father's name, Tom felt as though he had been punched in the gut. He stared at the ground, trying to calm the sick feeling in his stomach.

"Are you all right?" asked Daltec gently.

"We saw him," Elenna explained. "Taladon was there, on the Isle of Ghosts. Malvel, too."

Aduro frowned. "Malvel?"

Tom looked up and nodded. "We think he was behind it all. It was him who lured Berric there in the first place. He wanted to return to Avantia and..."

He tailed off. All the blood had

drained from Aduro's face, and the old man had begun to shake. "Did you touch him?" he asked, his voice little more than a croak. "Did anyone?"

"Berric did," said Elenna. "And Tom."

Aduro moved forward, resting a palm on Tom's head and closing his eyes. "I sense no evil in you," he said after a moment. "But where is Berric?"

"Don't worry," put in Captain Harkman. "He's in the dungeons. My men found him yesterday, wandering through the fields on his own. Tattered robe, filthy hair... He looked a sorry state!"

Aduro had already turned and was hobbling away, across the courtyard.

Tom and Elenna exchanged a glance, then set off after him.

Aduro led them through an archway, down a flight of steps and into the gloom of the dungeons, his purple robe swishing behind him. They passed down a corridor lined with barred doors, where prisoners peered mournfully from the darkness within. At last they reached the cell at the end, and all three of them stopped dead.

Tom shook his head, hoping his eyes deceived him. *It can't be...*

The bars were melted away,

leaving a hole the size of a grown
man. And beyond, the cell was
entirely empty.

"Just as I feared," muttered Aduro.

Elenna peered closer. "There's

something written inside," she said.

They stepped into the cell to investigate. Words were scored deep into the stone wall, as though by a sword, or a claw.

I TOLD YOU
IT WAS NOT THE END

A shiver ran down Tom's spine. "I don't understand," he said. "We left Malvel on the Isle of Ghosts. He's trapped there...isn't he?"

Aduro shook his head. "I wouldn't be so sure, Tom. If Malvel touched Berric, some of his dark spirit could have infected the young sorcerer. And if so, Malvel may have got his wish after all – he may have returned to Avantia, inside Berric. We must be on our guard."

"Wait," said Tom. "I touched my father. Does that mean his spirit is within me, too?"

Just as he spoke, Tom felt a strange warmth come over him, and a familiar voice whispered inside his head.

I will always be with you, Tom. You know that.

For a moment, Tom felt dizzy with shock. Then, slowly, a grin spread across his face.

Elenna raised an eyebrow. "I don't know why you're so happy! If Malvel is back, our Quest is far from over."

"That's true," said Tom. "But whatever he throws at us, we'll be ready for it."

My father, Elenna and me against Malvel...

He doesn't stand a chance!

THE END

CONGRATULATIONS, YOU HAVE COMPLETED THIS QUEST!

At the end of each chapter you were awarded a special gold coin.
The QUEST in this book was worth an amazing 8 coins.

Look at the Beast Quest totem picture inside the back cover of this book to see how far you've come in your journey to become

MASTER OF THE BEASTS.

The more books you read, the more coins you will collect!

Do you want your own Beast Quest Totem?

1. Cut out and collect the coin below
2. Go to the Beast Quest website
3. Download and print out your totem
4. Add your coin to the totem
www.beastquest.co.uk/totem

Don't miss the first exciting Beast Quest book in this series, ZULOK THE WINGED SPIRIT!

Read on for a sneak peek...

NOISES IN THE NIGHT

Tom jolted upright in bed, his heart pounding against his ribcage as he stared into the darkness. Black shapes lurked in the shadows, hunched like crouching Beasts. As Tom's eyes adjusted, the menacing forms became nothing but a chair draped with clothes, his nightstand, the brass fireguard. His pulse began to slow.

But what woke me?

Tom shivered and reached for the sweaty blankets tangled about his legs – then froze. A piercing cry filled the night. He leapt from his bed. *Someone's in trouble!* Tom grabbed his sword and dashed from the room. Then he heard the cry again, from somewhere above.

Cold flagstones sped beneath Tom's feet as he followed the corridor. The sound led him up a staircase, down a narrow passage then up more spiral stairs until he reached the door to the palace battlements. The terrible cry seemed to come from just outside. Tom thrust the door open, ready to fight. Instead, soft grey silence greeted him. The cry had stopped and dense fog hid the palace rooftops.

"Who's there?" Tom called. No one answered. As Tom stepped out, the fog wrapped around him, muffling his senses. The sharp tang of ice crystals hung in the air, nipping his nose. At first, Tom couldn't see more than an arm's length ahead, but then the fog swirled, revealing the ghostly shadows of battlements and towers. Something moved in the greyness – a tall, dark form. Tom tensed. It

looked like a cloaked and hooded
man, striding along the parapet wall.
Tom's heart clenched with alarm.
Nothing separated the strange figure
from a deadly drop on to cold, hard
stone far below.

"Are you all right?" Tom called, his
voice ringing strangely in the cold
air. "You should be careful up there."

The figure didn't answer, but
walked steadily away from him
into the mist. Something about the

figure's broad, straight shoulders caught at Tom's memory.

One of the king's men? But it seemed unlikely that Captain Harkman would post a watch with the king and queen away in Tangala. *An intruder, then?* Tom crept silently along the ramparts after the shadowy figure. His breath rose in white puffs before his face, mingling with the fog, and his bare feet soon turned numb with the cold. Once the figure reached the southern tower, it stopped and turned as if to gaze out over the hidden city.

"Hello!" Tom called. "Do you need help?"

The figure didn't move. Tom leapt

softly on to the rampart wall and crept closer. The air around him seemed to grow colder still, tingling in his chest and making his muscles knot and quiver.

"Easy there," Tom said, keeping his voice as calm and steady as he could. "Why don't we just step back down?" He drew so close to the hooded form, he could almost reach out and touch it – but something held him back.

"Tom!" a deep, commanding voice said. A fierce pang of emotion made Tom gasp and almost stagger. *Father!* The figure turned. Taladon's dark, piercing eyes looking back at him through the fog. Tom froze, his vision blurring with tears.

"Make haste to the Knight's Knoll," Taladon said, in a low, gravelly voice filled with urgency. "Do not delay!"

"Father, is it really you?" Tom

asked, longing to believe his senses.

"The Knight's Knoll, Tom," Taladon repeated. "You must not fail – Avantia depends on you." Tendrils of mist swirled around Taladon's figure.

"Don't go!" Tom cried, his chest heaving with emotion, questions crowding his mind. "What's at the Knight's Knoll?"

"Hurry, Tom, before it's too late," Taladon's voice echoed hollowly.

A wave of grief crashed over Tom, making his throat ache and his eyes burn. He reached for his father, then his stomach gave a sickening lurch as his heel met no resistance and the solid brickwork dropped away...

"Tom!" Firm hands gripped his

arm, steadying him, pulling him back. It was Elenna, her brows pinched together with concern. "You almost fell off the roof!" she said.

"T-T-Taladon!" Tom stuttered through chattering teeth. His while body shuddered with cold, though the strange chill had left the air. "Didn't you see him?"

Read
ZULOK THE WINGED SPIRIT
to find out what happens next!